Carnival Kids

Lucas Kavner

A SAMUEL FRENCH ACTING EDITION

SAMUEL FRENCH

FOUNDED 1830

SAMUELFRENCH.COM
SAMUELFRENCH-LONDON.CO.UK

FOR PRODUCTION ENQUIRIES

UNITED STATES AND CANADA
Info@SamuelFrench.com
1-866-598-8449

UNITED KINGDOM AND EUROPE
Plays@SamuelFrench-London.co.uk
020-7255-4302

Each title is subject to availability from Samuel French, depending upon
country of performance. Please be aware that CARNIVAL KIDS may
not be licensed by Samuel French in your territory. Professional and
amateur producers should contact the nearest Samuel French office or
licensing partner to verify availability.

For all enquiries regarding motion picture, television, and other media
rights, please contact Di Glazer, ICM Partners, 730 Fifth Avenue, New
York, NY 10019.

MUSIC USE NOTE

Licensees are solely responsible for obtaining formal written permission from copyright owners to use copyrighted music in the performance of this play and are strongly cautioned to do so. If no such permission is obtained by the licensee, then the licensee must use only original music that the licensee owns and controls. Licensees are solely responsible and liable for all music clearances and shall indemnify the copyright owners of the play(s) and their licensing agent, Samuel French, against any costs, expenses, losses and liabilities arising from the use of music by licensees. Please contact the appropriate music licensing authority in your territory for the rights to any incidental music.

IMPORTANT BILLING AND CREDIT REQUIREMENTS

If you have obtained performance rights to this title, please refer to your licensing agreement for important billing and credit requirements.

CARNIVAL KIDS was first produced by Lesser America in association with Claire Siebers at The Barrow Group Theatre in New York City on June 5, 2014. The performance was directed by Stephen Brackett, with sets by Meredith Ries, costumes by Tristan Raines, lights by Amith Chandrashaker, and sound by Janie Bullard. The Production Stage Manager was Kevin Clutz. The cast was as follows:

DALE	Randall Newsome
MARK	Jake Choi
ECKLAND	Max Jenkins
MARISA	Laura Ramadei
KALINA	Danelle Eliav

CHARACTERS

DALE – 50s. Texan.

MARK – 20s. Asian-American. Dale's adopted son.

ECKLAND – 20s. Mark's roommate.

MARISA – 20s.

KALINA – late 20s/early 30s. Syrian.

SETTING

Mark and Eckland's Morningside Heights apartment in New York City.
Also one scene in a bar, one in a public park,
and two scenes in Marisa's bedroom.

AUTHOR'S NOTE

A "/" indicates the point where the next character's dialogue should begin.

A note on Eckland's music:

The first production of this play incorporated original music that was specific to the needs of that production. Licensees are encouraged to create original tracks for production usage. If there are any questions, please reach out to the playwright's agent for assistance. See copyright page for contact information.

Scene 1

(Lights up on **MARK** *and* **ECKLAND** *'s Morningside Heights apartment.)*

(It's small. Dorm-like. Nothing really homey about it.)

(A living room connects to a small kitchen, with a dining table.)

(There's a couch facing an unseen television.)

(Two doors connect to two unseen bedrooms.)

(This place has been IKEA-ed to the max, without much warmth or care.)

*(***ECKLAND** *sits facing the TV. He has a headset on, playing a video game with a group of others online.)*

(He's intensely focused.)

ECKLAND. I know, but there's gonna be a million Soviets either way we look, so uh Packrat and, uh, SkaRus, is that SkaRus up there?

OK you guys, you guys stay on the machine gun up top and we'll go in to the factory.

The fac – wait, who's talking?

Who's talking right now?

OK, you gotta – you gotta say your name.

FlizzMasta.

FlizzMasta, you need to take that field behind the barracks otherwise we're gonna get flanked, we're gonna be smeared on toast like a bunch of sluts.

Does everyone have ammo?

7

Blinker, you can get like 20 rounds in the kitchen if you head back there.

> (**DALE** *opens the front door and peers into the apartment.*)

> (*He carries one giant suitcase and a small, battered laptop case and a couple of plastic bags filled with stuff.*)

> (*He drops it all on the floor, sweating profusely.*)

I have one grenade, does anyone else have grenades?

What about mines?

What about –

Mines.

How many?

OK, who's – who is *talk*ing? Who is talking right now?

Predator, you and Slingz sound exactly the same, does anyone else notice that?

They sound like the same guy.

Do you guys have the same Indian mother? Are you little secret Indian brothers?

> (**ECKLAND** *laughs.*)

> (**DALE** *just stands in the doorway. He's not quite sure what to do.*)

> (*He places his suitcase somewhere sort of out of the way.*)

ECKLAND. Skizzles.

Fliprocks, Millcat. Slings9.

That's four, that works.

OK, gentlemen, we ready to maulllllll?

DALE.
Hey I'm sorry is Mark here –?

OK… Go. GO. GO. GO.

ECKLAND. Millcat stand behind me, stop firing in my face.

Hey, don't – no no no nononono don't stop moving.

Fliprocks are you behind that bush or in the house?

SHIT, fuck, no.

DALE. Hey man, is / Mark here?

ECKLAND. *(to DALE)* One sec, one sec.

(back to game) Brazzles.

Brazzles.

BRAZZLES.

Aaaaaah, what are you doing in the *house*, you need to come out here now we're –

Aaaaah shit, someone needs to find that sniper now goddamn it, he's killing EVERYONE.

Do you see him?

Do you see the fucking SNIPER, BRAZZLES?

DALE. Hey, is it alright / if –

ECKLAND. There is nobody back there, Brazzles.

You're WASTING YOUR TIME IN THE LAUNDRY ROOM, BRAZZLES.

I'm getting shot.

I'm getting shot right now.

I'm getting –

I'm dead.

I'm out.

Goddamn it.

(beat)

DALE. Hi, sorry to bother you, are you Eckland?

ECKLAND. Yeah I'm Eckland.

You're Mark's dad?

DALE. I am.

ECKLAND. *(to headset)* Back in an hour.

(He removes his headset and stands.)

(a moment)

DALE. Is Mark here?

ECKLAND. He's still in class.

DALE. Told me he'd be back round 2:00.

ECKLAND. What time is it now?

DALE. *(checks his watch)* 2:15.

> *(beat)*

ECKLAND. You're, uh…

You're a white guy.

DALE. That is…true.

ECKLAND. Sorry, just 'cause –

DALE. Don't worry about it.

ECKLAND. Did you pick him up from, like, *Asia* or…?

DALE. Did we pick him up?

ECKLAND. I guess they probably flew him out to you.

DALE. We picked him up from Dallas. 'Bout a twenty minute drive from our house.

ECKLAND. Oh, OK, so he's Asian but not *officially*.

…

Is that your luggage?

DALE. Yeah, this is the battalion for now. Might ship a few boxes up from Frisco.

ECKLAND. Cool, so…welcome to your new house!

Mi casa es…your casa.

Or whatever.

DALE. It's just a short while, I promise.

ECKLAND. Yeah, well, it is what it is.

What it is, what it izzz.

> *(short beat)*

So do you want me to show you where things are? Like, a tour or…?

> *(**DALE** nods, stands.)*

OK so…this is the living room.

> *(He holds his arms out.)*

Where we're standing.

DALE. Right, figured that.

ECKLAND. The couch folds out.

Actually, we can…

Here.

(He starts to try and unfold it.)

It's kind of – ahhh, crap, sorry, it's kind of hard to do right now.

(They clumsily unfold the couch into a bed together.)

(It's already got some thin looking sheets on it.)

(They look at the bed together.)

I'm sure Mark got you a pillow, bigger blanket and stuff.

DALE. This is fine right here.

ECKLAND. So the living room connects to the kitchen, which is to our right, and it basically has everything a kitchen would have.

(He opens cabinets.)

Plates are here, cups are here, forks and spoons and everything are in here, and the – oh, the toaster is broken, doesn't work, but Mark doesn't want to get a new one 'cause he says he never uses the toaster, which is *bull*shit.

DALE. Why don't you just buy a new one?

ECKLAND. Huh?

DALE. Why don't you just buy a new toaster?

ECKLAND. 'Cause it's *his* toaster.

(short beat)

Rent up on the fridge every month. Or wait, are you paying Mark or is Mark paying your share or –

DALE. Me and Mark worked that out.

ECKLAND. Oh right, he said something about – I guess you're paying like 300 for the couch and then our rents will go down a little to correspond with that?

DALE. That sounds right.

ECKLAND. OK, yeah, money's not really an object for me right now, so...

*(**DALE** picks up a picture frame and looks at it for too long.)*

(Then he puts it down.)

Did you hear what I said or –?

(DALE shakes his head.)

I just said money isn't really a problem for me right now, so...

DALE. Is there laundry?

ECKLAND. Like in the building or in the neighborhood or...?

DALE. Just curious where I should do my laundry.

ECKLAND. Oh, cool, so yeah, I drop mine off at this place down the street. It's called like Pat's or... Cat's. I can't remember. But you can just drop it off and wait like a day, two days, depending on how busy it is and then you pick it up, and then at that point they've already folded it and everything.

DALE. OK, but if I just want to do some here are there machines in the building?

ECKLAND. Yeah, in the basement.

...

But if you go to this other place they'll fold it all for you and make sure it fits in your bag.

It's a little more money but I hate doing laundry, so...

I don't know if you hate doing laundry.

DALE. Been doing it about 35 years now.

ECKLAND. Oh right, so you're probably...pretty good.

But this place down the street gives you Tootsie Rolls while you wait and I kinda like stuff like that, like little things like that.

DALE. Hey, can I smoke out that window there?

ECKLAND. Oh, uh –

DALE. Or I can go downstairs.

ECKLAND. No, you – uh...

Yeah, sure.

(ECKLAND opens the window a crack.)

(DALE goes to it and lights a cigarette.)

(a pause)

So do you have friends in the area?

What are you going to, like, do all day?

DALE. Make some money. That's the plan.

Maybe see the Empire State Building.

Take a carriage round the – whatsit, Central *Park*.

ECKLAND. Those are expensive.

DALE. *(half a joke)* Well, you got any friends who wanna pay an old guy a few thousand bucks real quick?

ECKLAND. Like, for work, or...?

(an uncomfortable moment)

(Then the key in the door turns.)

Oh, there he is.

(DALE stubs out his cigarette real fast as MARK appears in the doorway, overdressed for the hot day, like always.)

DALE. Marky!

MARK. Hey dad.

DALE. Marky Mark!

(DALE moves in for a hug.)

MARK. Sorry I wasn't here when you got in, I had to talk to my professor for a sec after class.

DALE. That's alright Marky, real glad to see ya.

MARK. Yeah, you too.

You met Eckland?

DALE. Yeah, he's been showin' me around.

MARK. Great, great.

DALE. He showed me your toaster –

ECKLAND. I showed him the broken toaster.

(short beat)

DALE. Hey, you're sweating all over! Take off your coat, have a seat.

MARK. It's hot out today.

DALE. Well, hotter probably 'cause you're wearing a big ol' coat.

That's the culprit there.

Let me –

> (**DALE** *reaches to take it off,* **MARK** *backs away slightly.*)

MARK. Oh, I'm about to head back out, so I'll just – I'm OK, actually.

DALE. You sure?

ECKLAND. *(loudly)* Hey, I'm gonna go.

MARK. What?

ECKLAND. Oh, I'm gonna go.

Into…my bedroom.

So.

DALE. Well, nice meetin' ya.

> (*He shakes* **DALE**'s *hand.*)

> (*Then stands there a second.*)

> (*Another moment and he goes.*)

MARK. He's…

Sorry about that.

DALE. Nah, don't worry about it –

MARK. He was a friend of a friend, I didn't know he'd be so… *(gesture to suggest "a lot")*

DALE. Is Eckland his first name?

MARK. It's actually his middle name, he says it sounds more *professional*.

DALE. Huh. OK.

MARK. He's exceedingly rich, Eckland. He probably mentioned that a few times.

DALE. Oh, hey, well, maybe he can throw me a bone, then!

MARK. *(laughs)* Yeah –

DALE. Two bones!

> (**DALE** *laughs. Then a silence.*)

(gesturing to the boring apartment) So hey, look at *this*, huh? Marky's New York bachelor pad!

You ought to put some shit on the walls.

MARK. I kind of like it clean.

DALE. Hey, you know what I was thinkin' about? That place we went with your mom last time I was here. That Middle Eastern place with the hummus and that big fat cat runnin' around.

MARK. Oh, God, yeah, that place was terrible.

DALE. I thought it was pretty good!

MARK. There's way better Middle Eastern in the area, round here.

DALE. Well we should eat that, too! Let's go grab a bite, ya know, I want the full *palette* of the city, the full, uh – Big Apple *taste* courtesy of Marky Mark!

MARK. Tonight's actually pretty rough for me? I've got a bunch of work and I'm teaching an undergrad class on top of the paralegal stuff, so –

DALE. Wait.

You're teaching?

> (**MARK** *smiles, nods.* **DALE** *loves this.*)

Holy shit! So does that make you a pro*fessor*?

MARK. Yeah, sort of.

DALE. Oh, man! How 'bout that.

MARK. Yeah, it's been lots of work, lots of grading, you know.

DALE. Well, that's just amazing.

MARK. Thanks.

DALE. Real proud of you, Professor Ennis.

> *(short beat)*

MARK. Did you talk to Mom?

DALE. Uh…haven't for a lil while, no –

MARK. OK, yeah, I talked to her yesterday just to fill her in –

DALE. Uh oh!

MARK. No, no, not a bad thing, not bad. *(laughs)* She just wants you to call her at some point.

DALE. I thought she was in *New*foundland or some fuckin' place…

MARK. That was last month. This month she's in Senegal.

DALE. Senegal?

MARK. Yeah, in Africa. She said Carl's doing some work with a bank up there.

DALE. *Sen*egal, holy shit –

MARK. They're staying with a local family and eating goat, apparently.

DALE. Eating *goats*. OK!

Shit.

Well good for them, right?

MARK. Totally, um, *(checks his phone)* so I gotta run pretty soon? But I got this chest of drawers for you, so you can stick clothes in there.

> (**MARK** *taps a small, clear plastic chest of drawers in the corner, like something from the Container Store, set up next to the couch.*)

DALE. Chest o' drawers, great. Love these things.

MARK. Towels in the bathroom cabinet. And I've got some granola bars in the pantry, but you're welcome to grab a few groceries and stock up with whatever.

DALE. Perfect. That's perfect.

MARK. Do you have a suit? Something you need to hang up?

DALE. Uh, not at the moment, no. It's back in storage. I'm gonna have Mike ship it out along with a few other things, once I get another place.

MARK. OK, 'cause you have some interviews coming up, right? Like job interviews?

DALE. Definitely! Definitely. You remember Pat Hauser? He owned ABC Copies on Coit, you met him a couple times? Well, he's got a friend who works in corporate for Kinko's, and he's gonna get me in there very, very soon.

MARK. Awesome! That's great. So we'll have to get you some...

I mean, you're going to need to dress up for those interviews, right?

DALE. Yeah, I'm planning on making a big purchase like that soon as I can, but maybe in the meantime I can go ahead and borrow something nice from you, like some *slacks* or something?

MARK.	**DALE.**
Oh, uh, yeah, that's –	We're about the same size, yeah?

MARK. What?

DALE. *(a joke)* We're about the same size, you and me?

MARK. Yeah, I mean...

You really didn't bring anything like that with you?

DALE. Nah, but I'll be fine.

I'll be alright.

> (**MARK** *nods, meekly.*)

> (**DALE** *goes to him.*)

Hey.

Marky.

> (*He takes* **MARK**'s *head in his hands.*)

It's real good to see your face.

Alright?

That's all.

It's good to see your face.

I'll go to that department store I saw on the way over here.

Fuh-leens or wherever. I'll go there, pick something up. Don't worry about me.

    (**MARK** *breaks away.*)

MARK. Cool! OK, um, I might be back a little late tonight 'cause I'm meeting an old friend from high school for a drink? But –

DALE. OK, so if I have questions or I need to reach you should I, / uh…

MARK. Just call if you need anything, I'll have my phone.

DALE. Cool, great news, so is there a landline here or…? Maybe there's a payphone nearby?

    (*short beat*)

MARK. You don't have your cell phone?

DALE. Oh no I got it, I just – I gotta get a new charger for it? 'Cause right now you plug it in and the, uh, the battery doesn't…

But I'm gonna run and get a new one soon as I can.

MARK. Alright! Cool. We'll talk tonight, OK?

DALE. Alright, see ya then, Marky. See ya then.

MARK. Yup, see ya.

    (**MARK** *nods again, grabs his bag and starts to quickly head out.*)

DALE. Thank you.

    …

For doing this.

    (**MARK** *nods quickly and exits.*)

    (**DALE** *just sort of stands there a moment.*)

    (*We hear* **ECKLAND** *in his bedroom, faintly, watching a British sitcom.*)

    (**DALE** *goes to the pantry and grabs a granola bar.*)

(He takes a bite, wanders the apartment.)

(He picks up that picture frame again, and then he puts it down.)

(He walks to the couch, his new bed, his new room, and he sits for a long moment.)

(Music. Light change.)

Scene 2

(Later that night.)

*(**DALE** is curled up on the couch and asleep, with a trade paperback on his chest.)*

*(**ECKLAND** enters the kitchen with sandwich ingredients he has brought from his bedroom. He flicks on the light, forgetting that **DALE** is sleeping on the couch.)*

*(He starts to prepare a sandwich and **DALE** stirs, startling **ECKLAND**.)*

ECKLAND. Ah – shit.

DALE. *(groggy sounds)*

ECKLAND. Sorry, I totally forgot you were there.

DALE. S'ok.

*(**DALE** rubs his eyes. Beat.)*

ECKLAND. *(whispering)* Do you want some kale chips?

DALE. Some what?

ECKLAND. *(still whispering)* Kale chips.
   It's just kale –

DALE. Nah, I'll just – I'm OK, thanks.

ECKLAND. I gotta put a reminder in my head that you're sleeping here, that's my oops.

DALE. Your what?

ECKLAND. Oops. It's my oops.

*(**DALE** shuts his eyes and lays back down again.)*

*(After a moment, **ECKLAND** drops a giant jar of mayonnaise on the ground.)*

*(**ECKLAND** quietly reaches down to pick it up.)*

*(Realizing he's not going to fall asleep, **DALE** stands and heads to the kitchen for a glass of water.)*

ECKLAND. I Googled you.

DALE. Hm?

ECKLAND. Oh, sorry, I Googled you? Like an hour ago.

DALE. Oh, alright.

ECKLAND. I can't believe Mark never said anything about your whole...

I mean, you had a real band! You were like really real, in *magazines* and stuff.

DALE. Yeah, for a few years there we were...really real.

ECKLAND. Your music's on fucking Spotify!

DALE. Oh yeah?

ECKLAND. Yeah you guys have, like, four of your albums on there, and that one song on the, uh, the Fleetwood Mac tribute thing? You're on there with Elvis Costello and John Prine, and what was that picture of you on the vinyl from your second album?

DALE. I don't know –

ECKLAND. The one where you're like, mounting the neon trees? *(He goes to his laptop.)* Here, I'll look it up.

DALE. Maybe later.

ECKLAND. I'll just search it real fast.

DALE. Not right now, OK?

Maybe later.

> (**ECKLAND** *grabs his laptop, opens it.*)

ECKLAND. Carnival Kids. Did you guys, like, hang out at a fair or something?

DALE. It's a long story.

ECKLAND. You have a Wikipedia page with personal info.

DALE. Personal *info.*

ECKLAND. Yeah, come on, you never Google yourself?

DALE. Not recently, no.

ECKLAND. That's lies. Everybody Googles themselves, and plus you were in a real band, so you definitely have to Google yourself like all the time.

DALE. Guess I haven't gotten around to it.

ECKLAND. I'd Google myself all day if I was in a real band like that.

But hey, you know, c'est la vie right?

DALE. C'est la vie to what?

ECKLAND. You know, just to…

> *(He trails off.)*

Hey, but while you're living here we should definitely play.

I mean, I do mostly beats? But I have like three Roland 620s in my room, which you'll love, 'cause you played keys, you'll love them, and I collect synths and OH! You have to see some of these Moogs I found on eBay last year. They're all in this studio space I'm building, we can head / over there –

DALE. *(amused now)* You're building a studio?

ECKLAND. Hell yeah, I'm building a studio in Harlem so we definitely have to jam out while you're here.

DALE. I dunno if I'll have time to do that.

ECKLAND. You don't know if you'll have *time?* What else are you doing?

> *(short beat)*

DALE. How are you affording all this, huh? Your Moogs, the studio space –

ECKLAND. Oh it's from the app.

It's all app money.

> *(**DALE** shakes his head, confused.)*

Oh, I figured Mark…

I made a bunch of money on this app I created and I've kind of been riding that for a while.

DALE. What do you mean *app* money?

ECKLAND. Like money from the app I made.

> *(**DALE**'s still confused.)*

OK.

So apps, right? You know how iPhones have apps?

DALE. Sure, well I know what the...

I've seen an iPhone work.

ECKLAND. Right, so the little... I guess, the – *(laughs)* this is so funny! To explain this. Um, the little *boxes?* Those are the apps. It's an abbreviation.

DALE. Oh, right, right.

ECKLAND. For applications?

DALE. I see.

ECKLAND. That's so funny I've never had to explain apps.

DALE. Well, I'm a little older than you, Eckland.

(short beat)

So what does your app do?

ECKLAND. It's called GambleUp.

DALE. OK, and what does it *do*, what's its *func*tion?

ECKLAND. You download it and you can bet on stuff with people all over the world. Anything from sports to what the weather will be tomorrow to, like, how many times a politician says "America" in a speech, you know? Anything. And it's not in the app store, you have to find it illegally, but it's been downloaded a whole lot.

DALE. How much?

ECKLAND. Over four million downloads so far.

DALE. Four *million.*

ECKLAND. Yeah, it's craaaaaazy, I can't even deal with how crazy it's gotten. And this is just the first version, we'll have another one out later this year.

DALE. And how much do people pay for it?

ECKLAND. Per download? A dollar.

DALE. And how much of that goes to you?

ECKLAND. Well I split a percentage with other designers, but...

A lot.

DALE. Just say.

ECKLAND. Just a lot.

DALE. Say the number.

ECKLAND. I made six hundred and thirty thousand dollars last year.

> *(beat)*
>
> (**ECKLAND** *takes a proud bite of his sandwich.*)

DALE. Wooo.

ECKLAND. Yeah.

DALE. Jesus Christ. What the hell are you still doin' here?

ECKLAND. I'm probably moving out soon. Just getting my ducks in a row. Um, but if you have any app ideas, like any at all just shoot 'em my way, definitely.

DALE. Sure, I'll do that.

ECKLAND. Yeah 'cause hey, you need money right?

> *(short beat)*

You need money. That's why you're here, yeah? 'Cause you're out of money.

> (**DALE** *says nothing.*)

Right?

DALE. I don't want to gamble on your app, man.

ECKLAND. I don't want you gambling on my app either, but there's this other one that I think could be really good for you, it's really easy.

DALE. Well, I'll take a job if you got one. You need any employees for a new app thing, or other companies you got goin' –

ECKLAND. No, not at all. But you could make like ten grand doing basically nothing with GreenWay.

DALE. From what?

ECKLAND. GreenWay. It's easy, I know someone who just did it.

DALE. Oh yeah, yeah, and can I work from home, too?

ECKLAND. I'm serious.

DALE. I don't need your internet pyramid bullshit.

ECKLAND. No, listen, it's not that, OK? You just meet a nice person, you be charming for a few weeks, you make ten grand. It's like Tinder, except instead of looking for someone to date, you're looking for someone to get married to...so you can get them a green card. GreenWay. You wanna see?

> (**DALE** *shakes his head.*)

Come on, can I just show you?

DALE. Just leave it alone, man.

ECKLAND. Come on, I'll do this for you, I'll help you with this, if you just play some music with me for like...five minutes.

Howbout that, huh? That's all I want.

Five minutes. Ten grand.

> (**DALE** *hesitates, then slowly moves to sit back down at the table.*)

> (*He looks at the laptop.*)

Perfect!

Great.

OK.

So...first question:

How old are you?

> (*Lights.*)

Scene 3

(A wine bar off right or left. Low music plays.)

(MARK sits with MARISA, who is like that smart, intense girl from your high school English class who discovered alcohol and sex in college.)

(She is dressed for a desk job.)

(They drink beers.)

MARISA. That's a lot of hours.

MARK. Fingers crossed it leads to a full-time job, that's the only reason I'm doing the paralegal thing, 'cause the firm is perfect.

MARISA. I'm sure it'll work out, you're super smart.

MARK. Thanks.

MARISA. Super smart and so driven and blabblablablah. Fuckin' valedictorian up in here, right? Let's not forget.

MARK. No, no. Not quite –

MARISA. Oh *shit*, I forgot. The *controversy.*

MARK. Chris Cobb...

MARISA. Chris *Cobb*, oh God, I haven't thought about him in fucking *years*, Chris Cobb and his striped shirts, you guys and your little thing, your little rivalry. What were you, like two decimals behind him?

      (very quick beat)

MARK. Point oh three.

MARISA. Point oh *three*, of course.

But come on, you didn't want valedictorian anyway. You would have hated giving that speech.

MARK. Would I?

MARISA. Yeah, you would have obsessed over it, driven yourself totally insane. Plus we'd already had like three Asian valedictorians in three years, so, you know, it was nice to give that awkward white gentleman a shot.

A little affirmative valedictorian action, right?

(MARK smiles.)

You're gonna be fine. You'll be valedictorian of the law in a couple years and Chris Cobb is probably...he's probably dead, right? Let's be honest.

MARK. I actually think he's a lawyer in Baltimore.

MARISA. Oh, shit, that's perfect.

(MARK checks his watch, surreptitiously.)

You about done here?

MARK. Hm?

MARISA. That's like the third time, / you – *(indicates watch)*

MARK. Oh no, sorry, it's just, uh, I got someone staying with me for a bit –

MARISA. Who?

MARK. My dad.

MARISA. Oh, like for the weekend?

MARK. Uh, it's sort of indefinite right now.

MARISA. Woah.

MARK. Yeah, he kind of lost his job.

MARISA. Oh, that's rough. Like recently, or –?

MARK. Two years ago.

MARISA. Oh.

Shit.

MARK. Yeah, it's pretty complicated, we don't have / to –

MARISA. He came all the way from Texas?

MARK. He said he needed to get out of there and he rented out our house, the house I grew up in, and now he's here.

Um, but we don't really...

We're not very close, I guess, so... it kind of feels like I'm housing a middle-aged man for a recession *aid* program.

MARISA. Except it's your dad –

MARK. I know, / but –

MARISA. You're not just going to let him die.

(short beat)

You gonna help him find a job?

MARK. Yeah, for sure. That's the plan.

But he didn't even…

I mean, he didn't even bring a pair of *khakis.*

Like to meet people, to meet potential employers, he didn't bring anything to wear.

(short beat)

MARISA. Oh God.

MARK. But you know what / I mean?

MARISA. Not. A *one* pair.

Of khakis.

MARK. OK –

MARISA. I'm going to throw up on this table.

MARK. That's not what I meant –

MARISA. Get that man out of your house. For the good of America, get him out.

MARK.	**MARISA.**
The point is more –	This is America right?

MARISA. A man with no khakis! In *America!*

MARK. I get it.

Thank you.

MARISA. Aw, I'm just fucking with you, Mark.

I gotta say, it's nice to see you *affected.* By something.

MARK. What do you – how do you mean "affected"?

MARISA. Just, you know…

MARK. What?

MARISA. It's nice to see some sort of emotional…

I mean, we e-mail once a year and you only talk about school and *internships* and things like that, I never really hear anything else from you.

MARK. OK but what do you mean it's nice to see / I'm *affected* or –

MARISA. I mean you never talk about who you're dating, who you're hanging out with, what you *feel* about...

In your emails you write these short pointed sentences. You've always been like that, everything so suc*cinct* and agg*ressive.*

You're like Hemingway.

You're Hemingwang.

MARK. *(mildly offended)* Huh.

MARISA. That's actually pretty funny.

MARK. Yeah, that's a good one.

MARISA. So, like, who are you sleeping with?

> *(short beat)*

You don't sleep with people in law school? There's no sex with people?

MARK. No I mean there's...

Obviously.

MARISA. Obviously what?

MARK. I haven't seen you in three *years.*

MARISA. So?

> *(They look at each other.)*

> *(**MARK** sips from his drink, anxiously.)*

God, you're still so *funny.*

MARK. Yeah, well you're –

MARISA. I'm still funny, too?

MARK. No, you just...you have the same *spark.*

MARISA. I was kind of sad then and I didn't really like myself.

I feel pretty different now.

MARK. Good, that's... Good.

> *(short beat)*

MARISA. So hey.

What is this?

MARK. What's what?

MARISA. This.

Are we on a date?

MARK. Um.

MARISA. Are we on a romantic date?

MARK. I didn't think about it.

MARISA. I was G-chatting with Sam Crawley this afternoon –

MARK. Oh, wow. / Is he still…?

MARISA. And I was like, "I'm hanging out with Mark Ennis tonight, he asked me to hang out and we're going to have a *drink*," and it suddenly seemed so fucking *weird*.

MARK. Why do you think that's weird?

MARISA. Why do I think it's weird…

Hm, why do *I*

think it's weird…

Because the moose, Mark.

MARK. The…

What?

MARISA. The moose.

On your windshield.

       (**MARK** *stares at her, blankly.*)

Fuck. Really?

MARK. Oh, yeah, yeah, I remember that –

MARISA. You don't, you don't remember –

MARK. Yes, I do.

MARISA. What did it say? In the antlers?

MARK. I know what it said.

MARISA. I bet you do.

       (*laughs*)

Wow!

That shit was my heart!

My heart, Mark Ennis.

       (**MARK** *doesn't know what to do, so he just smiles.*)

       (**MARISA** *stretches, shakes it off.*)

Wow, Fridays just bonk me out, you know, *one* drink and I'm... *(gesture to indicate passing out)*

(beat)

MARK. Hey, look I'm sorry about the moose thing. Is that what this is...?

MARISA. Is that what what is?

MARK. I just thought this would just be, like, a catch-up session or whatever, so / I'm sorry I didn't...

MARISA. This is a catch-up session.

MARK. Yeah, it's really fun, I just –

MARISA. It is fun, it's a *fun* catch-up session.

MARK. Maybe this is a date.

Howbout that?

(short beat)

MARISA. When was the last date you went on?

MARK. *(thinking)* Um...

MARISA. Oh, come on.

MARK. I don't know, maybe a year ago?

MARISA. What was her name?

MARK. It was this girl Al? Or Andie. Something short for Andrea.

MARISA. *Al* or *Andie?*

(MARK *nods.)*

A year ago, you went on a date with a girl named *Al* or *Andie* but you're not sure.

MARK. Yeah...

(beat)

MARISA. Mark.

MARK. What?

MARISA. *Mark.*

MARK. *(unsure how to respond)* What?

MARISA. You wear *nice* ties.

You're going to be rich.

It's not un*reason*able to think…

MARK. *What?* What are you even…?

MARISA. You just seem to me, and I don't know this for sure, so fuck it, but you seem like you're so stuck in this sort of…

> *(She makes a container motion with her hands, trying to find the word.)*

It seems hard to operate. Inside of there.

MARK. I operate *fine.*

MARISA. K, nevermind.

MARK. You know, this was supposed to be a nice thing I was doing.

MARISA. It is nice, it is *very* nice of you to spend time with me, I'm sorry –

MARK. I just wanted to talk about what was going on in our lives, you know? I was happy to see you.

MARISA. You're not happy to see me anymore?

MARK. It's not that –

MARISA. Why, 'cause I'm asking you questions?

MARK. No, it's just –

MARISA. Because I'm *chall*enging you?

MARK. You're *brut*alizing me.

MARISA. Asking you questions about your life, about your personal life, is brutalizing you?

> **(MARK** *eats a large handful of party mix on the bar. He chews.)*

We go through life, and we…

You were im*portant* to me.

MARK. You were – yeah, you were important to me, too.

MARISA. Yeah.

Was I?

Never mind. Don't answer that.

So hey my mom died, right?

Six months ago.

MARK. Oh.

I'm –

I didn't know –

MARISA. Of course you didn't know, why would you?

(short beat)

Sorry.

I just keep thinking that even if I'd found out all these things I wanted to know about her before she died, which I didn't, I never even came close, I don't think I ever really cared about her…nature?

Like who she really was to everyone else.

I mean. I *did*, but not really.

(short beat)

Do you know what I mean, though?

That feeling?

MARK. That we don't care about each other's natures?

MARISA. That we *think* we do, but really we're just tossing all these rings out, you know, like we're tossing them out everywhere, trying to snag a bottle, but you can never really catch it all the way, you know? I mean, maybe one time if you're really lucky, but…

Not usually.

Usually you miss.

*(**MARK** nods, not quite sure what she means.)*

I want to see a real side of you.

MARK. Yeah. Me too.

MARISA. Because I'm interested in you, Mark.

I always have been.

MARK. Yeah.

Me too.

…

I want to see you, too.

(a moment)

(**MARK** *takes a sip of his beer.*)

(**MARISA** *looks at him as he struggles to hold eye contact.*)

(*Lights.*)

Scene 4

(The park.)

*(**KALINA** sits on a bench, playing with her cell phone.)*

(She wears a mix of traditional Syrian clothing and modern, hipster clothing.)

(She is immediately striking, and speaks with a slight accent.)

*(**DALE** wanders on.)*

(He's out of breath, having been running to get here.)

(He wears a cowboy hat, or something like it.)

*(**DALE** looks at a printed piece of paper, still breathing heavily. Then he turns around and makes eye contact with **KALINA**.)*

(He stares for a moment, trying to make sure it's her. She doesn't really help him, she just kind of stares back. Finally, he goes to her.)

DALE. Hey, uh…
    Kah-linna?
    Or…

KALINA. Kaleena.

DALE. Kaleena, hi.

(They shake hands.)

Sorry I'm a little late. My train did a crazy, uh…how come the trains run on different lines like that?

KALINA. How do you mean?

DALE. Like I'll be riding on the A train and all of a sudden it'll turn into the F out of nowhere.

KALINA. Oh, yes, it does that.

DALE. But why don't they warn you about it? On the, uh, on the speaker –

KALINA. There was no notice on the platform?

DALE. No! None. They just… *(gesture of a subway zipping by)* I mean, I asked the guy next to me how they can just switch it up like that and he says I should use *Hopstop* to find out when the, uh, the trains are on, when they're running on different lines.

KALINA. That's a good idea.

DALE. Is that a book or what?

KALINA. Is what a book?

DALE. Is Hopstop a *book* or a place I'm supposed to go or –?

KALINA. Oh, it's a website. And an app.

DALE. Ah, an app. 'Course it's an app…

> *(a moment)*

KALINA. How old are you?

DALE. I'm 50.

Two.

I'm 52.

KALINA. For some reason on GreenWay the dates –

It didn't / seem…

DALE. Yeah, sorry –

KALINA. I'm 28.

DALE. Aw, that's a fun age. That's a good year, 28.

> *(beat)*

KALINA. I like your hat.

DALE. Oh yeah? Thanks, I really like…all you got on there.

KALINA. Thanks.

DALE. You do fashion right?

KALINA. Costume design.

DALE. And that's for any kind of…? Various costumes or…

KALINA. For film or TV or theatre.

DALE. Right, so you gotta be pretty quick with a machine. With one of those, uh…with a sewing machine.

KALINA. Yes.

DALE. Or I don't know, maybe you don't use sewing machines anymore. What do y'all use now?

KALINA. Sewing machines.

DALE. OK, so those are still…operational.

> *(short beat)*

KALINA. What do you do?

DALE. I… What do I do. That's an interesting…

Well.

I was a musician. For a long time.

Toured around the world, that whole thing.

And then I met a woman, this lovely woman, a *teacher*, and I fell in love and we got married and we adopted a boy, a son, and I had to quit playing music, you know, so I could actually make money, or make more than just breaking even. So I opened a repair shop and then a print shop and then I tried music again for a hot second and it didn't feel the same so I went back to the print shop. And then the print shop went out of business, so then I tried to sell some things I thought were worth a lot of money, but none of that clicked.

And, so uh…

Now I'm here. In the city.

Talking to you.

> *(short beat)*

KALINA. You just provided a lot of information.

DALE. *(laughs)* I guess so, yeah.

KALINA. That was like your whole life right there.

DALE. You're from, uh…

> *(He takes out his piece of paper.)*

Damascus?

What's that like? How's Damascus?

KALINA. Well.

It's pretty fucked up right now actually.

DALE. Oh right, that's right, / I'm sorry –

KALINA. It *was* very nice. Before… / everything –

DALE. Right, before the war and such, yeah.

But your family is…?

KALINA. My family is fine, my immediate family. We all left.

I'm the only one who came here, though. To New York.

DALE. Wow, that's impressive.

KALINA. I like it here.

DALE. Yeah, this place makes you feel young, you know? Except I'm already kind of sick of the walking, honestly.

(*He laughs at that.*)

Why don't we all just use scooters? It'd be so much faster.

KALINA. I have a friend with a scooter but everybody makes fun of him.

DALE. Well, they shouldn't 'cause he's got the right fuckin' idea.

Or, sorry – that's not –

KALINA. What?

DALE. The swearing. Shouldn't waste that on a beautiful woman.

KALINA. That's OK, I did it earlier.

DALE. No, you didn't.

KALINA. Yes, I did. I said 'Syria's pretty fucked up right now.'

DALE. Get outta here.

KALINA. I say shit and fuck all day.

DALE. Jesus! Don't do that.

KALINA. It's OK.

DALE. With your pretty accent, it feels weird.

KALINA. Fine.

I won't swear anymore.

DALE. Good. That's good.

KALINA. No more fucking swearing.

(DALE *laughs.*)

(KALINA *smiles, wryly.*)

(*a moment*)

DALE. So what do you got, like ten people coming to meet you today? You're gonna cycle through us?

KALINA. You are the only one I'm meeting today.

DALE. What about yesterday?

KALINA. Yesterday...

Yes. I met some others.

This is marriage.

My life, all my future.

Can I ask you a question?

DALE. Sure.

KALINA. Are you a Republican?

DALE. What?

KALINA. Are you a Republican?

DALE. I'm – what? Why do you think that?

KALINA. Your accent sounds like you could maybe be a Republican.

DALE. Well, that's very xenophobic of you, Kalina.

KALINA. You're right, I'm sorry –

DALE. I didn't ask if you were a terrorist.

KALINA. ...And I'm very happy you did not.

(*The tone changes, just a bit.*)

(*an awkward beat*)

But I must ask a couple other things, just because they'll ask us these as part of the application process.

First. Have you been convicted of a crime?

DALE. I was in jail for one night.

In Cleveland, Ohio. In 1982.

KALINA. Why?

DALE. I stole a massage chair from a hotel lobby.

KALINA. A massage chair?

DALE. Yeah, you know, one of those chairs that vibrates and
pounds your back.

KALINA. You are funny. I'm laughing inside.

And you have a son, you said?

DALE. One son. Adopted.

KALINA. Adopted. Why?

DALE. 'Cause I'm infertile.

(short beat)

KALINA. I see.

DALE. But that's OK for us, right?

KALINA. Yes, I think so –

DALE. 'Cause we're not having kids.

(beat)

Let me ask you something, though?

Why are you doing it this way? Don't you have like a
friend or someone who can go through this whole
thing with you?

KALINA. I haven't been in the city long enough, all my
friends are in my position.

DALE. Alright, / but –

KALINA. Look, this is not an easy process. We will need
to learn everything about each other, our families,
histories, our first dates. They are going to ask for
photographs and scrapbooks and proof that we've
spent time together.

DALE. So how do we do all that?

KALINA. Photoshop.

(short beat)

The computer program.

I have a friend, he will help make our history with
Photoshop.

DALE. Jesus.

KALINA. But that's only if I pick you, Dale.

   ...

   If I pick you to be my husband.

DALE. Well.

   You got my vote.

> *(He salutes or something, like Uncle Sam.)*

> *(***KALINA*** *smiles.)*

KALINA. I'm going to take our picture.

> *(She pulls out her iPhone and scoots closer to* ***DALE.****)*

> *(He takes off his hat.)*

> *(She takes a selfie.)*

> *(She looks at it and smiles.)*

DALE. Why are you smiling?

KALINA. We look nice.

DALE. Lemme see.

> *(She shows him.)*

   Shit, is that what I really look like?

KALINA. Let's take another.

DALE. Alright, lemme put the hat back on.

> *(He does.)*

> *(They pose again.)*

> *(Lights.)*

Scene 5

(**ECKLAND** *and* **DALE** *sit on his fold out couch.*)

(*There's a synth keyboard in front of them. They're sharing a pair of headphones.*)

(**MARK** *sits on the table, working on his computer. He watches them.*)

ECKLAND. You hear that? You hear that resonance?

DALE. Yeah, that's real clear. Wow.

ECKLAND. Now listen when I mess with the Cutoff.

(**ECKLAND** *turns a knob on the keyboard.*)

(**DALE** *smiles.*)

DALE. Oh yeah, that's cool.

ECKLAND. Isn't that sick?

(*He tweaks the knob again.*)

(*making a sound*) Meeeooooo. You hear that? Meeeeooooo.

When I play live, like sometime in the next few months, maybe, that's the plan, if my friend Chiara can play E-drums? But for the live gigs, I'm just gonna use this one board.

Like just this one.

(**DALE** *listens, gives* **ECKLAND** *a thumbs up.*)

You ever hear resonance like that before? When you were playing?

DALE. I mean I was never into anything super digital back then. I was always playing a Rhodes, you know, so –

ECKLAND. Wait, like a full-blown Rhodes?

DALE. Yeah, full blown.

ECKLAND. (*finds this uproarious*) Oh my God! That's fucking insane!

DALE. Yeah, we were nuts.

ECKLAND. How did you *lift* it?!

DALE. It was goddamn heavy, I'll tell you that. Our roadie wanted to shoot me in the head.

ECKLAND. But they sound so good so that's the tradeoff.

DALE. Nothing sounds like a Rhodes, man. Never will.

ECKLAND. Wait, listen to this.

> (*DALE listens on the headphones.* **ECKLAND** *plays a few notes for him.*)

DALE. Is that a dog barking?

ECKLAND. Oh wait, no, that's not what I…

> (*He presses some buttons, plays the notes again.*)

Here, now listen.

> (**DALE** *listens.*)

> (**ECKLAND** *waits with baited breath.*)

You don't recognize that?!

DALE. Am I supposed to?

ECKLAND. That's an actual Rhodes, man! I filtered the sound from an E.L.O album. Took me like eighteen hours to get it right, but…it's pretty close, isn't it?

MARK. Hey, dad?

> (*headphones still on*)

ECKLAND. It's pretty close. Like the tone is close.

MARK. Dad?

ECKLAND. Oh, Mark's saying something.

DALE. (*headphones off*) What's up, Marky?

MARK. Sorry, I just, um.

I found a couple Craigslist posts for jobs I thought you might like? If you wanted to –

DALE. Oh yeah?

MARK. Yeah, one's with a licensing company, like for music and commercial licensing? I thought that might –

DALE. Oh, yeah that could –

MARK. Another is for this bar, like scheduling shows? So
    you'd work / in the –

ECKLAND. Your dad's got a job.

> *(short beat)*

MARK. He…what?

ECKLAND. He's got a job.

> (**DALE** *and* **ECKLAND** *exchange a quick look.*)

DALE. Yeah…

    I got a job. So, you don't have to worry about that.

MARK. What's the – what is it?

ECKLAND. He's doing the score.

    For this new app I'm designing.

    Making all the music.

MARK. Oh, wow. That sounds cool.

ECKLAND. Anyway, if you turn the resonance up super
    high, it's more synth-y but –

MARK.	**ECKLAND.**
What kind of music is it?	If you take it out completely, it's sort of like a horn? Like brass?

DALE. What's that, Marky?

MARK. What kind of music are you going to write?

DALE. It's, uh –

ECKLAND. It's like dreamy, kind of ambient rock stuff. Very
    '70s. Your dad was perfect for it.

MARK. And it's a decent salary?

DALE. Uh, well, that's sort of / up in the air –

ECKLAND. It's a ten thousand dollar stipend.

    Initially.

    But then later, if it sells well, he'll get more.

    Do you want to hear a completely realistic helicopter
    sound effect?

DALE.	**ECKLAND.**
I don't know, is that –	It sounds real.

MARK. So you're all set for money then?

DALE. Yeah Marky, I'm all set. Maybe we should go out and celebrate, huh? What're you up to tonight?

MARK. I'm going to see a friend.

Actually it's that friend I saw the other night.

DALE. Oh, nice.

Is this a girl or...?

MARK. It is, actually.

It's a girl I'm seeing.

DALE. Hey, very cool! That's very cool, when can I meet her?

ECKLAND. What's her name?

MARK. Marisa.

DALE.	**ECKLAND.**
Marisa, that's great.	I don't know her.

MARK. So then I guess you're gonna start looking for other places? Now that you got this money all set?

ECKLAND. I'm just gonna turn this off 'cause you guys are talking.

(*He goes to unplug the synth.*)

DALE. I'd kinda like to stay here a bit longer, if that's OK, just 'cause I don't really have the money yet –

ECKLAND. Yeah, I can't really pay him *yet*.

(*short beat*)

MARK. Uh huh.

Yeah, I mean...that's cool.

DALE. You sure?

MARK. Yeah, no, of course. It's totally fine. So I guess you'll make this ten grand and you'll be able to pay the rent for this place and maybe some of what you still owe Mom, and then you'll be able to rent a place of your own? With what you have left over?

(*short beat*)

DALE. That's the plan.

MARK. Cool.

> (**MARK** *packs up his computer, grabs his jacket.*)

DALE. I'm also planning a few interviews for…just like a
  couple weeks from now. Got the Kinko's thing coming
  up. But this'll tide me over.

MARK. Perfect!

DALE. You headin' out now?

MARK. Yeah, gotta run a few errands.

DALE. OK, you need help with anything, or…?

MARK. No, it's OK! Have fun, see you guys soon.

> (**MARK** *leaves in a hurry.*)
>
> (**DALE** *stands by the door.*)
>
> (*a moment*)
>
> (**ECKLAND** *waits and then slowly plugs the synth
> back in again.*)

ECKLAND. Pretty good save, huh? With the job thing?

DALE. Yeah, real good save.

ECKLAND. I just figured…since your chances looked pretty
  good with the GreenWay, might as well get ya off the
  hook.

> (**DALE** *nods.*)
>
> (**ECKLAND** *puts the headphones back on.*)
>
> (*Lights.*)

Scene 6

(MARISA's bedroom.)

(Later that night.)

(MARISA sits on the bed.)

(MARK has their old high school yearbook open.)

MARK. "Keep it real, keep it cool, never falter.
Peace. Mitch."

MARISA. Poetry.

MARK. Were you and Mitch Feriss even friends?

MARISA. No, God, no, I literally walked up to him on the last day of school and asked if he'd sign it.

MARK. Why?

MARISA. 'Cause I wanted a hot guy to sign my fucking yearbook.

MARK. That's weird.

MARISA. Oh, you think that's out of *character* for me?

MARK. Maybe.

MARISA. You're in it, too.

(He flips around. She gets up and helps.)

There.

MARK. "Hey Marisa, this was a good year. Hope to see you very soon."

(short beat)

MARISA. It seethes with feeling.

MARK. *(soaking in his words)* "This was a good year.
Hope to see you very soon."
God.
I mean that's...

MARISA. I remember what I wrote in your yearbook.

MARK. Really? Like, exactly?

MARISA. Yes, Mark. Every *word*.

No, I just remember I took a whole page. I made you reserve me a page, you know, like we did, and I took it all through fifth and sixth periods and I wrote out all these drafts on pieces of notebook paper and I sketched out your name all…girl-like, or whatever. Like your name in big letters on the top of the page. But then I didn't end up using that one.

MARK. Why?

MARISA. 'Cause I figured you'd think it was too *girly*, or something.

MARK. My name in letters on a page would seem girly?

MARISA. Immature.

I don't know.

You intimidated me back then.

MARK. I think I would have said it was cool.

MARISA. You would not have said it was *cool*, Mark, but whatever, I wrote something nice.

> (**MARK** *has flipped to a page and a bunch of photographs fall out.*)

> (*He looks at them.*)

MARK. Oh man, those suits.

MARISA. Remember when we went to that tournament at Taft Point and you got first in Oratory and that very pointy girl was stalking you the whole day?
Who *was* that?

MARK. I don't remember –

MARISA. Oh come on. She cornered you in the cafeteria and made you discuss gun control legislation. She wanted to S your D so bad, I thought I'd turn a corner and you'd be, like, going down on each other behind the popcorn machine.

> (**MARK** *just sort of smiles and nods.*)

> (*He looks at another picture.*)

MARK. Woah, you took this? I don't remember this.

MARISA. Yeah, right after graduation.

That's your dad, right?

MARK. Uh huh.

> *(He looks for a long beat.)*

MARISA. OK!

So, do you want to watch something or –?

I mean what do you want to do?

Why ya *here*, Mark?

MARK. *(cracks a smile)* Uh…

MARISA. No offense, I just mean…you asked to hang out again, / so.

MARK. I know, that's true.

MARISA. It is true.

MARK. I don't know.

I was thinking…

Like…

> *(**MARK** slowly, probably too slowly, moves in to kiss her, his neck outstretched. They kiss for a little bit.)*

MARISA. Ha.

MARK. Is that OK?

MARISA. Yeah, it's cool.

> *(He kisses her again. She kisses back.)*

> *(Then he very deliberately begins to remove **MARISA**'s shirt, one button at a time.)*

> *(They are not kissing while he does this.)*

Mark.

MARK. Hm.

MARISA. *Mark.*

> *(She takes off her shirt.)*

> *(She tries to move faster but he struggles to keep up.)*

(She takes off his shirt quickly and they get under the covers.)

(He starts to touch her below the belt and it's way too aggressive.)

(We can see his arm moving way faster than it should.)

Holy Jesus.

MARK. What?

MARISA. Are you pumping a bicycle tire?

MARK. Sorry –

(She takes his hand and has him go slower.)

*(**MARISA** closes her eyes, **MARK**'s remain open.)*

*(Then **MARISA** takes off **MARK**'s pants.)*

*(**MARK** struggles to take off **MARISA**'s.)*

*(We see pants wriggle out from under the sheets, as **MARK**'s coins and wallet and cell phone fall out of his pockets.)*

Oh crap –

MARISA. It's OK.

MARK. All the stuff / just –

MARISA. *(re: phone)* It's not broken.

MARK. I know.

(They kiss a bit, like this, half-naked.)

*(**MARISA** reaches down again, under the covers.)*

MARISA. *(nicely, to his penis)* Come on now, buddy.

(a beat)

MARK. I'm sorry.

MARISA. It's OK.

(She touches him more.)

MARK. Shit.

MARISA. Is this gonna...? Should I keep going?

MARK. I don't know.

I'm sorry.

> (**MARK** *stands up and walks to the corner.*)

> (*He stands there, back to the audience, looking down at his penis.*)

MARISA. Mark?

> (*beat*)

This is weird, will you come back here?

MARK. Just give me a second.

> (*He touches himself softly.*)

MARISA. Come back here, Mark.

MARK. Not yet, just let me...

MARISA. Please.

MARK. Just give me a second please.

MARISA. Come back into the bed.

Come back.

> (*Finally, defeated, he does.*)

> (*They lie there, on their backs.*)

MARK. I want to do this.

MARISA. OK.

MARK. That's why I came over.

MARISA. You came over because you wanted to have sex?

> (**MARK** *doesn't respond.*)

Well, alright then.

MARK. I thought you wanted this.

MARISA. I did.

Sort of.

I mean, I do.

> (*He turns to her again.*)

MARK.
　　Can we try again?

MARISA.
　　Have you ever done this before?

MARK. What?

MARISA. This.

> *(short beat)*

> (**MARK** *says nothing. He trembles.*)

You're shivering.

Do you know that you're shivering?

Like your whole body is –

MARK. I'm not shivering.

MARISA. You are, you're shivering like crazy.

MARK. I'm not cold.

> (**MARISA** *rubs his arms back and forth, trying to warm him.*)

> (*A low light remains on them…*)

Scene 7

*(That same night, in **MARK** and **ECKLAND***'s
apartment.)

*(***DALE*** *sleeps on the sofa bed.)*

(A knock at the door.)

*(***DALE*** *doesn't stir.)*

(Then another knock. Louder.)

*(***DALE*** *finally gets up, goes to the door.)*

(He looks through the peephole.)

*(Then he scrambles. He quickly re-folds the bed into
the sofa. Then he pulls on his pants and opens the
door.)*

*(***KALINA*** *stands there.)*

(She looks strung out, high or drunk on something.)

KALINA. Hello.

(beat)

May I…?

DALE. Oh, uh, / sure –

KALINA. Or I can leave.

DALE. No, come in.

(She does.)

What time is it?

KALINA. It's late.

*(***KALINA*** *wanders the apartment.)*

You have nothing on your walls.

It's very plain.

DALE. Yeah, I don't like the clutter.

KALINA. Can I have some water please?

DALE. Yeah, 'course.

(He goes to get her a glass of water.)

KALINA. I saw a man on the street tonight.

This cowboy man.

He had these two holsters.

I don't know if he was going to a costume party or he was a real cowboy just wandering the streets of New York.

But I thought of you.

DALE. A cowboy man.

KALINA. Mmhm.

*(A moment as **KALINA** gulps down her water.)*

DALE. That's good drinkin'.

KALINA. You're wondering how I found you.

DALE. Maybe a little.

KALINA. You gave me your address. The other day I asked for your contact info and you didn't give me a phone number, just an address.

DALE. Did I?

KALINA. *(laughs)* You're just, like…this Amish person.

So I wanted to see you in your natural habitat.

I wanted to see this man who came to meet me in a park with his sweaty shirt and accent in his natural habitat.

DALE. I wasn't so sweaty.

KALINA. You were very sweaty.

And you smell like something burning?

DALE. What's burning?

KALINA. No, I mean you smell like something is *burning*. Like your body smells like something burning in an oven, has anyone ever told you that?

DALE. That I smell like something burning?

KALINA. Yes.

DALE. Nah, haven't heard that one.

I've heard sweat and cigarettes, but not something in the oven.

That's a new one.

(Suddenly, **ECKLAND** *bursts out of his room holding a bat.)*

(He sees **DALE** *but not* **KALINA**. *)*

ECKLAND. Did you hear that knocking?

DALE. Yeah, don't worry about it.

ECKLAND. Who was knocking?

DALE. Don't worry about it.

ECKLAND. Who was it?

KALINA. I don't know, we should investigate.

    *(***ECKLAND*** drops his bat, startled.)*

DALE. Sorry. This is Kalina.

KALINA. Hello.

    You are Dale's roommate?

ECKLAND. Who is this?

DALE. This is, uh –

ECKLAND. Wait, are you… *(quiet, to* **DALE***)* is this from GreenWay?

DALE. Yeah, we met on GreenWay.

KALINA. And now we are going to be married!

    (She takes **DALE**'s *arm in hers, linking it.)*

    (A moment as they stand there together.)

ECKLAND. Oh!

    Nice. Congrats.

DALE. I didn't know I'd been chosen.

KALINA. I decided just now.

    Do you accept?

DALE. Yeah.

    For sure!

KALINA. Oh, that is fantastic!

    Now we celebrate the engagement!

    What do we have for celebration?

ECKLAND. I have some streamers left over from New Year's!

KALINA. No, wait, you have to go back to bed now.

ECKLAND. What?

KALINA. You go back to bed, because this moment is for me and my husband-to-be.

(*short beat*)

ECKLAND. Um.

DALE. (*to* **ECKLAND**) Just give us a few minutes?

ECKLAND. Yeah, it's cool.

I'll just go back into my bedroom now.

KALINA. Nice meeting you!

ECKLAND. Yeah, nice meeting you, too.

Really fun time out here.

(*With a look, he heads back to his room.*)

KALINA. I'm excited about this! Let's toast.

(*She takes out a small bottle of whiskey from her purse. Takes a swig.*)

DALE. Woah. Uh…maybe we oughta go down the street, ya know, get outta here.

KALINA. That's my toast. Now you toast.

(*She hands the bottle to him.*)

(*He looks at it.*)

DALE. You don't fuck around.

KALINA. I do not fuck around.

DALE. Is this how you do it in Damascus?

KALINA. No, this is how I do it in New York City.

(*He takes a sip.*)

Take more, hubby.

(*She tilts the bottle back into his mouth.*)

DALE. K, that's good. That's good for now.

KALINA. Hey, so guess what I did?

DALE. What did you do?

KALINA. I listened to your music.

DALE. Oh. Wow.

KALINA. I listened to your music online and I looked at your old pictures and I soaked up your past like a *sponge.*

DALE. And you still want to marry me?

KALINA. It must be so funny.

DALE. What?

KALINA. To have done all that for that time and then all of a sudden it just *stops*, like it stops in its tracks. Was that funny?

DALE. It was…funny.

KALINA. I guess artists, or – people. They drop off the earth all the time.

Like where are all those kids from *Step by Step?*

DALE. From what?

KALINA. *Step by Step.* It was a TV show in the 1990s about the families, the two families –

DALE. I think I missed that one.

KALINA. And now I have no idea what any of them are doing. I wonder if thoe kids just sit around saying to their friends, "Hey, I was on *Step by Step.*"

They probably have other lives now.

Other things.

DALE. You watched that show in Syria?

KALINA. Oh, yes. It was dubbed.

We had all of the popular shows.

DALE. I like imagining you back then, little Kalina huddled near a TV with her family, drinking punch or whatever. That's a nice image there.

KALINA. I like imagining you back in Texas shooting bottles with your cowboy guns.

(a moment)

DALE. Hey, let's go to a bar, huh? Get outta here?

KALINA. Why do you want to leave so bad?

DALE. I just, you know, I don't want to wake my roommate.

KALINA. He's OK, he is a big boy. He will be fine.
　　I want to stay here.

　　　　　　(She slinks to **DALE**.*)*

　　　　　　(Literally, she slinks.)

　　　　　　(She wraps her arms around his neck.)

DALE. Hello.

KALINA. Say 'howdy.'

DALE. What?

KALINA. Say 'howdy' just one time.

DALE. You want me / to –?

KALINA. Just say it.
　　Pleeeeeaase.

DALE. You're a funny girl.

KALINA. Come on.

DALE. Alright…howdy.

　　　　　　(She smiles.)

　　　　　　(She kisses him.)

　　　　　　(He kisses her back.)

KALINA. You are the cowboy man.
　　You are, you are.

　　　　　　(She kisses him again.)

　　　　　　(She pulls him toward her room.)

　　Should we go to your room?

DALE. Nah, let's stay out here.

KALINA. I want to see where the cowboy sleeps.

DALE. I want to stay out here.

　　　　　　(He kisses her again, more intensely.)

　　　　　　(Lights.)

Scene 8

(It's after 2 a.m. now.)

*(**MARK** unlocks the door and enters.)*

*(He immediately sees **DALE** and **KALINA** balled up on the couch together.)*

(He tosses his keys on a surface and takes off his coat. He sits at the kitchen table.)

*(**DALE** stirs.)*

DALE. Hey, Marky.

(short beat)

What time is it?

MARK. Two something.

(short beat)

DALE. Just fell asleep.

*(**MARK** looks at him, and her. On the couch.)*

This is, uh… Kalina here.

(She stays sleeping.)

We met in the park the other day.

MARK. Mm.

DALE. She's real nice, really interesting. I think you'll like her a lot.

I've told her a lot about you.

*(**MARK** nods.)*

MARK. How drunk are you right now?

DALE. Mmm. I'm a little bit, a little bit, but not a lot.

Not a lot, alright?

MARK. OK.

DALE. Not a lot, I promise. I don't do that, this isn't *about* that.

(**MARK** *paces to the other side of the room, like he might leave.*)

(**DALE** *stands quickly, exposing himself naked for a moment.* **MARK** *puts a hand over his face.*)

(**DALE** *grabs underwear and frantically pulls it on.*)

Hey, OK.

Hey.

Marky.

MARK. *(quiet)* Jesus.

DALE. I'm sorry, Marky, listen –

MARK. You gotta go somewhere.

DALE. What's that?

MARK. Just go somewhere please.

DALE. Go where?

MARK. Wherever.

Just… Somewhere else. Bars stay open late.

Diners.

DALE. Hey, I wanna spend time with you. That was part of why I did this, you know, why I came here. So I could spend time with you.

MARK. You did this because you had nowhere to go.

DALE. I could've gone to a friend's place.

MARK. What friends?

DALE. I have *friends*, Mark, Jesus Christ. I have friends at home.

MARK. You know what? You can stay, I'm gonna go.

DALE. No, it's your / house.

MARK. It's fine, I'm gonna go.

DALE. Listen, I'm gonna make some money coming up, OK?

MARK.	**DALE.**
Uh huh.	I told you –

MARK. Eckland's job.

DALE. Eckland's *job*. That's right, Eckland's job. What do you think I'm doing? I'm not just sitting around here, I'm figuring it out, alright? That's what I'm *doing*. I am figuring it out.

> (**KALINA** *stirs.*)

> (Both **MARK** and **DALE** *watch her as she rubs her eyes.*)

KALINA. What time is it?

MARK. 2:23.

KALINA. Oh.

> (*beat*)

Is this another roommate?

> (*She reaches for* **DALE**, *who looks to* **MARK**.)

> (**DALE** *says nothing.*)

MARK. Yup. I'm the other roommate.

KALINA. How many of you are there?

> (*Short beat.* **MARK** *goes to leave.*)

DALE. Hey.
Wait.
Marky, this isn't –
Come on.
Marky, please stay, will you?
Stay here.
Do not leave, you hear me?
Marky, DO NOT LEAVE THIS HOUSE.

> (**MARK** *walks out the door and heads out into the night.*)

> (**DALE** *stands there a moment, breathing heavily, in his underwear.*)

> (*Then he shuts the door. He locks it.*)

(He turns to **KALINA**, *who is now wide awake.)*

(A look between them that shatters the lights.)

Scene 9

(MARISA's bedroom. The next morning.)

(MARK, in a shirt and tie, lies on MARISA's bed on his laptop. MARISA changes for work, moving between her bathroom and bed.)

MARISA. So are you gonna need a key? Or should we just meet in the city?

MARK. It'll only be a couple days.

MARISA. I'm happy for you to stay with me, honestly, it's just a little...you know.

MARK. He says he's about to make some money, so maybe he's going to leave, or move in with this girl, / or –

MARISA. Can't you just ask him to get a hotel?

MARK. No.
He can't a*fford* that, he can barely afford a phone charger.

MARISA. Or khakis.

(MARK glares at her.)

Look, he's clearly making your life uncomfortable, you should talk to him about it.

MARK. I'd rather just let it *pass*, I don't feel good about talking to him about it.

MARISA. You don't really feel good about talking to him about anything, it seems like.

(beat)

Why don't you call your mom and ask what she thinks.

MARK. Because it's not her job to deal with this anymore.

MARISA. Whose job is it?

MARK. It shouldn't be anybody's job, but he's in my house, so I have to deal with it.

MARISA. Maybe this girl – what's her name?

MARK. I don't know. Kameena, or something.

MARISA. Maybe she really wants to be with him.

Maybe she'll take care of him, you know? Maybe this is really good.

MARK. Yeah.

MARISA. Yeah…

Well.

You stay as long as you need.

Just buy me some beers or something.

> (**MARK** *just sits a moment. Staring into space.*)

> (*short beat*)

Rooooomiiiies.

Who'da thunk?

MARK. Pretty crazy.

MARISA. Super crazy.

> (**MARISA,** *in just a bra now, starts buttoning her shirt.*)

MARK. Is it OK, though?

MARISA. That you're staying with me?

Yeah, I mean, it's kind of funny.

MARK. My friend Matt has his brother staying with him right now, and you live right near school, so –

MARISA. So it's super *convenient.*

MARK. No, I just mean –

MARISA. It's fine.

I'm glad I can be here for you.

> (*She stands there still mostly unbuttoned.*)

> (*After a moment, gauging his lack of response, she decides to button again.*)

Let's hang out tonight. What would make you really happy to do?

MARK. You don't have to hang out with me.

MARISA. I want to hang out with you, so tell me what would make you happy.

MARK. I got a bunch of work, / so –

MARISA. We're not doing *work*, you fucking nerdball, what's something else?

MARK. I don't really feel like doing anything –

MARISA. Well, I want to do something and you're staying with me, so what do you want to do?

MARK. Uh.

I guess we could order take out and, like…eat it?

MARISA. Yes, eating it sounds great.

MARK. And then maybe we could just, like…sit and watch Animal Planet?

> *(short beat)*

MARISA. That's the best night I've ever heard.

MARK. Great.

MARISA. Gold.

MARK. I'm gonna go to class.

MARISA. Perfect.

> *(He moves to kiss her on the cheek. She lets him.)*

> *(Then he lingers near her face a moment longer.)*

> *(beat)*

MARK. Sorry.

MARISA. Why?

MARK. Mmm…

> *(He's still lingering there.)*

MARISA. Mark.

MARK. Yeah, / I know.

MARISA. There's no *law*.

There are no rules with this.

MARK. I know.

MARISA. You don't have to do anything.

> *(He touches her face or something.)*

Just go to class.

MARK. OK.

(He breaks away further, smiles at her again, and walks to the door.)

Shit, I have to stop home for a book.

MARISA. Maybe it'll be empty.

MARK. Yeah.

MARISA. Or maybe your dad left you a love moose on the table with a note from his heart.

(an uncomfortable beat)

Have the best day, Mark.

*(**MARK** smiles at her again and leaves.)*

(A thumping electronic beat drowns out the moment.)

(Into...)

Scene 10

(**ECKLAND** *is playing his music for* **DALE**.)

(*He has set up the two Rolands in the living room.*)

(*And a vocal mic.*)

(*He shuffles back from the computer to one of the keyboards.*)

(*The vocal line comes in: it's* **ECKLAND** *singing, heavily reverbed: "Fourth night. Right. Time to go into the light."* **DALE** *nods his head along with the beat.*)

DALE. *(over the music)* What are you saying there?

ECKLAND. "Fourth Night. Right. Time to go into the light."

DALE. Does that mean anything?

ECKLAND. No, no, it's just words. I just liked the way it sounded.

(**DALE** *nods.*)

Alright, so if you feel inspired, jam out a keyboard line.

DALE. Just with the beat there?

ECKLAND. Yeah, or do you wanna do vox?

DALE. What?

ECKLAND. *(wearing headphones)* DO YOU WANT TO DO VOX?

DALE. Nah I don't do vocal stuff, I'll do keys.

(**DALE** *starts to play a few notes, feeling out the instrument.*)

(*Then he begins to play something.*)

(*It sounds like a Fleetwood Mac keyboard line, but over a modern electronic beat.*)

(*Something about it is vaguely exciting.*)

ECKLAND. Holy shit, what *is* that?!

DALE. Hm?

ECKLAND. WHAT IS THAT YOU'RE PLAYING?

DALE. I don't know, I'm just playing around.

ECKLAND. IT'S AMAZING.

> *(He continues to play the keyboard riff.)*

> *(ECKLAND grabs the mike and starts to improvise other verses to his song.)*

> *(sings)*

THE LIGHT UNDER THE SUN.
IT'S CRYING THROUGH THE MOON.
NOW THE SEASON HAS BEGUN.
NOW IS WHEN WINTER COMES.
WINTER COMES
WINTER COMES –

> *(He adds an echo effect to his voice, then he loops those verse lines over DALE's playing.)*

> *(Then he grabs a tiny synth and starts adding very high synth notes to the mix.)*

DALE. Woah.

ECKLAND. WHAT?

DALE. I wasn't expecting that.

ECKLAND. IS IT TOO MUCH WITH THE HIGH OCTAVES?

DALE. It's your tune, man, do what you want.

ECKLAND. It's too much, shit, it's too much, I'll just let you take keys.
Keep that going.

> *(MARK enters the apartment and sees them playing.)*

> *(He quickly walks into his room.)*

> *(DALE hears the door shut and stops playing.)*

> *(The electronic beat continues to thump.)*

WHY'D YOU STOP?

DALE. I think Mark's here.

ECKLAND. I didn't see him come in.

DALE. I heard his door shut. Can / you –

ECKLAND. WHAT?

DALE. Can you turn the music down a sec?

> (**ECKLAND** *turns the beat down a few notches.*)
>
> (*We hear the "click" sound of the Mac computer volume.*)
>
> (**MARK**'s *door opens. He holds a textbook.*)
>
> (*He and* **DALE** *stare at each other a moment, neither one wanting to start a conversation.*)

Hey, Marky.

MARK. Just grabbing a book for class.

DALE. What time are your classes today?

MARK. I have two classes and then I'm meeting a friend tonight.

Shouldn't you be at work?

DALE. Yeah –

ECKLAND. This is work. For him.

He's working right now.

> (*short beat*)

DALE. Where have you been sleeping?

MARK. At a friend's house.

DALE. Oh.

Well are you gonna come back and stay here soon?

MARK. I don't know what my plans are.

DALE. You should come back here.

You live here.

MARK. No, I'm OK. It's under control.

> (*He exits swiftly back out the door. He locks it.*)
>
> (**ECKLAND** *still has his headphones on.*)

ECKLAND. Holy shit, this sounds so good. Oh man! You gotta –

Dale, you gotta listen.

DALE. Goddammit.

ECKLAND. *(headphones back on)* YOU GOTTA LISTEN.

DALE. Will you turn down the music?

ECKLAND. WHAT?

DALE. TURN THE FUCKING MUSIC DOWN, ECKLAND.

> (**ECKLAND** *immediately does.*)

> (**DALE** *starts to shake, or something else with his body, very visibly.*)

ECKLAND. Hey, uh.

Can I get you some water?

> (**ECKLAND** *clicks something on his computer, which activates the music again, all at once, just for a moment.*)

DALE. TURN IT OFF.

> (**ECKLAND** *immediately clicks it off.*)

> (**DALE** *stares at the floor.*)

ECKLAND. Sorry, that was a total accident, that last thing.

DALE. I need – do you have some aspirin?

ECKLAND. I um… I have Advil?

> *(He runs to the kitchen and opens a cupboard.)*

Or wait. Is ibuprofen OK?

DALE. Whichever.

ECKLAND. Sorry if aspirin is your preference, I think this is all we have, so…

> (**ECKLAND** *brings* **DALE** *two ibuprofen, which he pounds down.*)

> (*A moment as* **ECKLAND** *decides what to say or do next.*)

We can take a break if you want.

(beat)

*(**DALE** grabs his cigarettes and opens the window a crack.)*

(He lights up and inhales deeply.)

DALE. FUCK.

(He smokes.)

(a long beat)

ECKLAND. Do you want some, like, time alone or…?

(beat)

DALE. I just wanna be useful.

ECKLAND. OK.

DALE. Of use. To somebody.

ECKLAND. Yeah, I mean…

Yeah, of course. We all do.

DALE. All I wanted is to…

(laughs)

I mean…

He shows up here and I'm on the couch with this…

What the hell is *wrong* with me?

ECKLAND. Nothing.

DALE. You said this would be easy. A few weeks, ten thousand bucks, that's what you *said*.

ECKLAND. I know, And it will be –

DALE. You gotta understand. I need something to work out here.

ECKLAND. It will.

It's all gonna be…

It's gonna be good. I promise.

*(After a moment, **ECKLAND** puts his headphones back on.)*

(He plays something on his computer.)

(**DALE** *sits, smoking.*)

(*Lights.*)

Scene 11

(**MARK** *and* **MARISA** *in her bed, lying next to each other.*)

(*Animal Planet plays on her TV.*)

(*They eat Thai food and drink wine from crappy cups.*)

MARISA. Meercats are so neurotic.

MARK. Mm.

MARISA. They're like a bunch of little Jewish men.

MARK. Hm. That's not really what I'd go with, but –

MARISA. No, like if a bunch of little Jewish men had a colony, it would be a meercat colony, 'cause they're always, like, moving their heads around, looking around for danger.

MARK. Mm.
Yeah, I guess if you forced a bunch of small Jewish men to live in a hill colony made of tiny holes –

MARISA. Just running around.

MARK. That's a TV show right there.

MARISA. *Tiny Jews Running Around.*
I think Woody Allen made that already.

(*They watch.*)

MARK. When I was like six, I got lost at the zoo.

MARISA. Is this a meercat story or is this unrelated?

MARK. There were meercats at the zoo.

MARISA. OK, just making sure we're not moving away from meercats yet.

MARK. Yeah, I did one of those things where you think one guy is your dad 'cause he's wearing the same color shirt? And you just follow behind him for a while, but then he turns around, and he might as well be a monster, because it's obviously – it's not your dad. You've been following the wrong guy.

MARISA. Oh yeah, I used to do that at the supermarket with my mom. Waiting in line.

MARK. Yeah and I knew I was lost, but I didn't turn myself in to security or anything, I just very intently wandered the zoo, alone, for like seven hours.

MARISA. Jesus!

MARK. Yeah, I just walked in circles.

MARISA. So when did your dad find you?

MARK. The zoo was closing.

There was nobody left.

MARISA. Were you crying? I mean, were you losing your shit?

MARK. No.

MARISA. No.

MARK. Honestly, I don't remember ever crying.

Like, at all.

MARISA. You mean in the last few years or –?

MARK. No, I mean…

I have no personal recollection of shedding tears.

MARISA. That's insane, man.

What if I stabbed you in the hand?

MARK. No, physical pain wouldn't make me cry.

MARISA. What if I stabbed your hand and then told you you weren't gonna graduate law school?

MARK. Then…

Yeah, I would cry.

MARISA. At last! Your emotional G-spot.

(She pours some more wine for herself.)

So you're wandering the zoo not crying. How'd you find your dad?

MARK. Yeah, so the zoo's closing. There's nobody left. I'm just…sitting. On this bench alone. Then this security guy in a giraffe hat grabs me and brings me back to my dad who's waiting at the entrance. And he's there and he says sorry, he's very serious, and he grabs my hand.

And we start walking back to the car and I'm just thinking, like…

You were hoping I'd be gone.

You were hoping I would disappear.

> (*short beat*)

And then two years after that I walked in on him fucking our neighbor.

MARISA. Woah.

MARK. In our *kitchen*, he had her bent over the…

And I just watched until they turned around and saw me.

It was like a minute before they saw me, and I was little, I didn't know…

I just watched them.

MARISA.	MARK.
Why did you stay?	I remember sounds.

MARK. That's gross, but the *sounds* were…

I don't remember the image as much as what it sounded like.

> (**MARK** *zones out a moment. Then comes back.*)

Sorry. I don't know what that had to do with meercats, / but maybe it –

MARISA. Yeah, kind of a roundabout thing there.

Probably has more to do with…other things…

> (*a moment*)

> (**MARISA** *smiles at him, warmly.*)

> (**MARK** *pats* **MARISA** *on the leg, like he's slapping a friend on the back.*)

(*sighs*) Oh, Mark Mark Mark.

MARK. What?

> (*He keeps his hand on her leg. Looks in her eyes.*)

MARISA. Mark.

MARK. What?

MARISA. Stop.

Seriously.

MARK. Stop what?

MARISA. Stop pretending you want to fuck me.

MARK. …

I'm not.

MARISA. Yes you are, you keep, like, *sort* of touching me and making this weird face in the corner of your eye, OK? Let's just sit here and eat this food and talk about meercats for fuck's sake.

> (**MARK** *backs off.*)

> (*They sit in the silence a moment.*)

I just want you to let this be *easy*, OK? Just realize there's not a rule for everything and you can do what you feel like and everything will be fine.

MARK. Hey, thanks Mom.

MARISA. I'm not your mom.

Alright?

I am not your mom.

> (*short beat*)

> (**MARISA** *goes to the bathroom.*)

> (**MARK** *shifts.*)

MARK. Maybe I'm asexual.

MARISA. That's just the word we used in high school to describe our gay friends.

> (**MARISA** *returns from the bathroom to* **MARK**'s *look.*)

MARK. What?

MARISA. Yeah, remember, we all said Gabe Ambers was "asexual" and then he came out the next year when he went to college. Same with Mike Westal.

MARK. That's not…

MARISA. I'm just saying.

MARK. Yeah, well, that's a huge thing to just fucking *say*. To say to somebody just off the cuff...

MARISA. Well, have you ever...?

(She stops.)

MARK. What?

MARISA. Let's just watch the meercats.

MARK. Just say it.

MARISA. Nothing, I'm sorry –

MARK. Say what you want to say.

MARISA. I don't want to say anything.

MARK. Yes you do.

MARISA. I just wondered if it ever *occurred* to you. That's all. It doesn't seem unreasonable to ask.

(She watches the meercats.)

MARK. Why would I be trying to have sex with you? If I was...

Why would I be *staying* with you?

MARISA. I don't know, let's just...

(They watch.)

*(**MARK** turns to **MARISA** and then aggressively moves in to kiss her.)*

(She lets him for a moment.)

(Then she pulls away.)

No, God, don't –

MARK. I want it.

MARISA. No you don't.

MARK. I want it. Please.

(He tries again, but she pulls back harder.)

(She falls off the bed.)

(Slowly, she gets back onto the bed.)

(A horribly uncomfortable moment.)

(They watch the TV.)

(Lights.)

Scene 12

(A laundromat)

(KALINA *texts on her phone as two dryers tumble behind her.)*

(Then a call comes in.)

(Her ringtone is a current popular song.)

(She answers.)

(Her accent is entirely gone.)

KALINA. Hey, what's up?

Yeah, is it cool if I come borrow a few more pieces?

Just like a couple more of those orange tops you have in the costume closet there, and maybe some of that jewelry we used on the film?

Oh, the hat! *(laughs)* Obviously the hat. That hat is the shiiiiit.

We're rehearsing near Columbia through the weekend, so that would be real helpful. I dunno, some Chekhov thing. It's faculty, though, so the money's good.

(ECKLAND *appears near* **KALINA,** *holding his large bag of folded laundry.)*

(He sees her. She doesn't see him.)

Well, I'd love to see you and the girls so if I don't make Liz's maybe we could grab dinner or a drink some time soon?

Sweet.

K, I'll swing by tomorrow, cool?

K, later.

(She hangs up.)

(She checks her phone.)

ECKLAND. Hey.

KALINA. Hey.

(KALINA *looks to* ECKLAND. *It takes a moment,
but she finally realizes who he is. Her demeanor
shifts.*)

ECKLAND. What's going on?

KALINA. *(going back to her initial accent)* Oh, I'm just doing
some laundry.

ECKLAND. In a Laundromat? Nah, you crazy.

KALINA. Don't you have laundry in your building?

ECKLAND. I like the Tootsie Rolls.

(*He eats a Tootsie Roll.*)

Were you talking to Dale?

KALINA. Hm?

ECKLAND. On the phone just there?

KALINA. Oh, no, just my friend.

ECKLAND. He said you haven't been calling him back.

KALINA. Who?

ECKLAND. Dale. He said that he's been trying to reach you.

KALINA. Oh yeah. I've been very busy with work.

ECKLAND. I gotcha.

(*short beat*)

So what was that just there?

KALINA. Sorry?

ECKLAND. On the phone just there.

Are you a cop?

KALINA. What?

ECKLAND. Are you a police officer or something?

KALINA. No.

ECKLAND. So then why were you all, like, different on the
phone?

KALINA. What are you talking / about?

ECKLAND. When I just heard you just there, your voice was
different, you were all different.

KALINA. I think you must have misheard.

ECKLAND. No, don't do that, no, I didn't mishear.

KALINA. I'm not a cop, Eckland.

ECKLAND. Well then what the fuck?

KALINA. Just...don't worry about it, alright?

ECKLAND. He's doing this for the money, you know. Because he needs the money. So it's not fair if you're just bullshitting your way through this.

KALINA. I'm obviously not *bullshitting* –

ECKLAND. I'm serious. Tell me now you're going to pay him or I'm going to tell him everything.

KALINA. We like each other a lot and this is real, OK? It is very real, it is not a video game or anything like that, / it's –

ECKLAND. What does that mean?

| **KALINA**. | **ECKLAND**. |
| Never mind. | I know it's real, OK. |

ECKLAND. If it's real then it's also not real 'cause you were just being someone else. So it's not real if that's what you were doing.

KALINA. I'm seeing him in a few hours, we'll talk about it then –

ECKLAND. Just tell me why you were being a totally different thing!

KALINA. *(losing composure and accent)* Because I thought if he *falls* for me then...

I thought he might have more *sym*pathy, or something, I thought he would care more if I played this type of person, OK?

I don't know.

ECKLAND. What, so then you wouldn't have to pay him because he'd be, like, in *love* with you?

KALINA. I guess.

Sort of.

ECKLAND. What do you think, he has some sort of, like, Arab *fetish*?

KALINA. No, I just didn't want to be myself. I tried being myself at first and it felt weird, I felt uncomfortable. And then I tried doing something new and it was nice, and he was nice, and I don't know, it just *developed*.

(**ECKLAND** *sighs.*)

I need the card, OK? I need it.

It's my whole life.

Please.

ECKLAND. Why did you stop calling him?

KALINA. The other night when your other roommate came home, he kind of freaked out, and I don't know, I felt all weird, / and –

ECKLAND. Wait, when who came home?

KALINA. Your other roommate.

The Asian guy?

ECKLAND. You mean Mark.

Dale's son.

Mark.

(*A pause.* **KALINA** *steps back.*)

You know you're breaking the GreenWay terms of agreement.

KALINA. It's an illegal iPhone app, Eckland, I don't think there are terms of agreement.

ECKLAND. There are terms of agreement, I've seen them.

(*A moment. And then* **ECKLAND** *reaches into his pocket and takes out his checkbook. He leans on one of the laundry machines and writes a check.*)

Just take this.

KALINA. No, come on.

ECKLAND. He can't know you were using him.

Or, I mean, he knows you were using him, but he can't know you were playing him.

Just put this in your account and pretend it's from you.

KALINA. I can't do that.

ECKLAND. Yeah you can.

> *(He holds it out.)*

> *(She doesn't take it.)*

Come on. Just take the check, call him back, and then it'll all be over after you get the marriage certificate, OK?

> *(another long moment)*

Take it now.

> *(Finally, she takes the check.)*

See?

There you go.

Easy.

KALINA. Are you going to say anything?

ECKLAND. No.

No way.

He's my friend.

> *(He lifts his laundry bag and walks out.)*

> *(**KALINA** looks out after him.)*

> *(Lights.)*

Scene 13

(**MARK** *and* **MARISA** *stand facing out, on separate sides of the stage.*)

(*They hold phones to their ears.*)

MARK. I just think it might be best, you know? After everything –

MARISA. Uh huh.

MARK. My friend Chris' roommate is out of town for the week, so I'm just gonna board up there.

MARISA. Makes sense.

MARK. Cool, cool.

    …

Um.

Just about everything that's happened with us this past week and what you said last night about me being…

I'm just hoping we can forget all that, you know?

    (*short beat*)

MARISA. *Forget* it.

MARK. Yeah, you know, just…

Pretend it didn't happen.

Go back to…

Before.

    (*a very long pause*)

Cool cool, well, thanks again / for –

MARISA. A Moose for All Seasons.

"This class is pretty boring, but I think you're pretty great."

    …

We were reading *Man for All Seasons* in English class.

I wrote it in the antlers and I gave it to you.

MARK. …I know.

MARISA. I mean, you were *it* for me.

Back then.

And now you don't know who you are or what you're doing or how to be warm and caring, and you've just strung me along.

You've really hurt me.

>   (**MARK** *just stands there.*)

I hope you get that job you want.

I wish you great success.

>   (**MARISA** *hangs up.*)

>   (**MARK** *remains there a moment, bathed in light.*)

Scene 14

(The apartment.)

(DALE smokes a cigarette next to ECKLAND.)

(They look at his laptop screen.)

DALE. I just can't believe this program.
I mean, it looks like we've really been all these places.

ECKLAND. The backgrounds aren't really melded so well on this one –

DALE. Looks pretty good to me. It's me and Kalina upstate next to a frozen lake.

ECKLAND. Yeah, but look at this –

DALE. I mean, the coats and everything? Your guy even made it season-specific –

ECKLAND. You can see your outlines, though.
Right there, see? Kalina's head sort of blends into the blue of the sky.

DALE. You'd need a magnifying glass to see that, man.

ECKLAND. When you print them out and put them in the scrapbook, they'll see. These have to be perfect. I'll mess with them.

> *(ECKLAND takes the computer, DALE takes a drag.)*

DALE. I'm just glad she's talking to me again.
I was really fuckin' worried for a second there.

ECKLAND. Yeah, well…
She had a lot going on.
Hey can I have a drag?

> *(He passes ECKLAND the cigarette.)*

DALE. Had that Kinko's thing this morning. Guy I knew wasn't even there. Thought I was meeting my friend and then I end up with this bozo in a bowtie.
I told him I hated paper.

> *(ECKLAND laughs, coughs from the cigarette.)*

I think I told a fuckin' copy empire…that I hated paper.

(They laugh.)

*(The keys in the door turn and **DALE** quickly grabs the cigarette back and stubs it out.)*

*(**MARK** enters.)*

*(He sees **ECKLAND** and **DALE** next to the window together.)*

(He regards them a moment and then drops his stuff down.)

(He looks like shit.)

Hey there.

*(**MARK** goes to the kitchen, grabs a snack.)*

I said HEY THERE.

MARK. You guys having a business meeting?

ECKLAND. What?

MARK. A business meeting. About your job?

DALE. No.

I was just having a smoke and hanging with Eckland.

MARK. Did I say you could smoke in here?

ECKLAND. I told him it was OK.

*(**MARK** nods, takes a bite of a granola bar.)*

DALE. Where have you been sleeping?

MARK. That's not really…it's not your business.

DALE. Alright.

MARK. You can stay in my room, actually. If you want. You don't have to sleep on the couch.

DALE. That's your room, Marky.

MARK. You and Eckland have been getting so close anyway, you might as well sleep together at this point. You can jam out all the time, start a band together.

DALE. Alright, come on –

MARK. Start a band and have parties and invite some chicks over and fuck them, right?

Fuck a bunch of chicks, yeah?

> *(beat)*

DALE. You've never talked to me like that before.

Eckland's a big music guy, you know? We just like playing music sometimes.

MARK. I'm a music guy.

DALE. Oh yeah?

MARK. Yeah.

DALE. You've never been a music guy before.

But it's OK –

DALE.	**MARK.**
You do most stuff way better than I ever could –	What makes you think –

MARK. What makes you think I'm not a music guy?

DALE. I don't *think* it, you're just…

I mean, when you were little I took you to shows, you barely responded. Took you to see Van Morrison on your eighth birthday, you wanted to play Game Boy the whole time.

MARK. That's 'cause I was eight years old, how can you use that as an example?

DALE. When I played music around the house, you just stared off into space, you know, but it's OK, it's who you *are*.

> *(MARK takes a moment, and then plows into his bedroom.)*

> *(After ten seconds, he re-emerges with a giant box.)*

> *(He dumps it on the coffee table and takes each item out one at a time.)*

MARK. Alright, what's this one…

Carnival Kids in *Q Magazine*.

You talk about making a record with Al Breadlow, scrapping your West Coast tour because your drummer got sick. Right? He had some throat thing? But it got better.

And here's uh – some custom made guitar strap from Fender, with your fairground logo pressed on.

(**DALE** *takes the strap and looks at it.*)

You got your mugs. Your stickers.

There's this charity vinyl you guys are on.

You covered a King Crimson song for this one, right?

(*He holds up a record.*)

DALE. Hank Williams, I think.

MARK. Oh, right, but you covered King Crimson for something else.

DALE. I think a B-Side.

MARK. Right, right. Here's that one.

(*He holds it up.*)

What else…

(**MARK** *pulls out a big stack of CDs and tapes and vinyl records, including "Bright Pink Alice," the one* **ECKLAND** *mentioned with the neon trees on the cover.*)

(*He dumps them all out on the table.*)

Here's every single album you ever made. CD and vinyl. Cassette tapes.

I even have "Corrupticon," that political EP you never released. I've actually listened to it a bunch and I think a couple of the tracks are good, but the concept didn't make any sense. I mean, were you railing against the government or Reagan's policies or what was the deal there?

DALE. I don't know, to be honest.

MARK. Yeah, that's unclear.

Here's a t-shirt of you guys sitting on a blue mountain?
I don't know why you're sitting on a blue mountain –

DALE. Jesus, neither do I.

MARK. When mom moved with Carl I took all this stuff, I've listened to it all.

DALE. Oh yeah?

MARK. Want to hear a song? I'll sing your songs to you.

DALE. I don't need to hear a song, Marky –

MARK. Name a song.

DALE. Marky.

MARK. Name a song, come on.

DALE. Uh…
"Call A Situation."

MARK. *(sings – badly, but sincerely)*
CALL A SITUATION WHAT IT IS.
IT'S NOT THE WAY YOU THOUGHT IT WOULD BE.
BUT IS ANYTHING THE WAY IT SEEMS?

DALE. Hey. That's…
I like that.

MARK. Name another.

DALE. I dunno –

MARK. *(sings again)*
BEEN ON A BALANCE BEAM SINCE I WAS SEVENTEEN,
I DON'T KNOW WHERE THE SUMMER'S GO.
BUT I CAN'T BE IN THE SCENE, I'M LIKE THE BEAUTY QUEEN
WITH THE DEAD AND THE BONES IN THE HOLE."
That's "Dead and Bones."

DALE. I like that one.

MARK. I can sing all of them, you know that? I could sing the whole catalogue.

DALE. I didn't know you liked any of that –

MARK. I bet you have so many stories, you probably met so many cool people.
You could have kept going if you wanted. Been a teacher, a music teacher, right?

Fucking – sold pianos, taught at a *camp* or something, a music camp, instead of a print shop –

DALE. I tried to teach, they wouldn't take me.

MARK. When?

DALE. When you were fourteen, I tried to get a job teaching at that arts magnet school in Dallas.

MARK. How did you – what did you try?

DALE. I sent in an application, / I told them –

MARK. You sent in an application, you didn't follow up, you didn't call anyone, you didn't send a note.

(short beat)

You could have done anything you wanted, but you never even told me about any of the good stuff, you never tell me *anything*. Why did I get this sad guy every day, every *single* day, why didn't I ever get to hear the good stuff?

DALE. 'Cause I thought you didn't want to hear about any of that. You were smarter than me. / You were –

MARK. I was smarter than you?

DALE. I was happy when I played those songs, hanging with those guys for those years. But I was 28 and coming back from those last tours and your mom was home, and I still had to get shifts with Tom Porter, remember him? At his fuckin' hardware store?

I was working there between gigs 'cause even though we were doing all that touring I still had no money. None. Breaking even every time, and I knew we wanted a family.

MARK. Yeah, but you regretted it.

DALE. I didn't regret it.

MARK. You did. You tried to give me back.

DALE. I what?

MARK. Mom told me when I was six months old, like a couple months after you got me, you put me in a car and tried to take me back.

DALE. What?! No, that's –

There was one day, I was fucked *up*, I wasn't trying to take you *back*. Jesus, why the hell would your mom say that to you?

MARK. Because it was true, she said –

DALE. Well, that's a lie, that's bullshit, OK? I was fucked up and we were tired and at each other's throats and I put you in the car and said, "This is it!" Or something. I don't fuckin' remember, but I wasn't actually gonna do anything, I would *never* have fuckin' –

Jesus, all this time, you thought that? You really thought I would do that?

MARK. I don't know. Maybe.

I just always wanted to get more of you. I wanted to see the part Eckland sees and this – whoever that girl is. What she sees.

I always got the broke and the drive around Texas for a few days without telling us where the hell you were and the drunk at the print shop and the *kitchen*.

(short beat)

DALE. OK.

I didn't enjoy that, do you hear me?

MARK. You didn't *enjoy* that?

DALE. You walking in on me like that? / Of course I didn't –

MARK. Twice. *Twice* I walked in.

DALE. Twice, yeah, twice, you think I enjoyed that?

MARK. I don't know what you enjoyed, but we've never talked about it so how am I supposed to know –

DALE. I didn't enjoy that. I didn't enjoy doing that to your mom or to you.

MARK. You didn't enjoy fucking people on the table in our kitchen? On our couch? You didn't enjoy that?

*(**DALE** shakes his head.)*

(long beat)

I can't even touch a girl, I can't even…

I don't know what's wrong with me.

DALE. Nothing's wrong with you.

MARK. I don't know how to *be*.

I don't know how to…

(**MARK** *starts to cry.*)

DALE. Is that my fault?

Mark?

That can't just be me, Marky –

MARK. I don't know whose *fault* it is, I'm just saying I don't know how to *be* with someone.

DALE. Well, maybe it's just 'cause…

You've always been *closed*, haven't you?

Just a little bit closed off from people and…not lettin' anyone in too deep, you know. That's always been part of your personality.

MARK. Where did I get it from?

Mom's not closed, you're not closed.

DALE. Maybe –

I don't know…

MARK. What?

DALE. Maybe you got it from your parents, Marky. Maybe you got it from the people you came out of.

(*short beat*)

Certain qualities nobody can explain.

People are who they are –

MARK. You're my parents.

DALE. I know that.

MARK. You're my parents.

DALE. I know.

MARK. The people I came out of, I don't know them.

DALE. I know, I didn't / mean to –

MARK. You're the one who's supposed to help me, to figure out what I'm supposed to do and who I'm supposed to be and how I'm supposed to be and now my whole life / you've –

DALE. That is not what I mean, Marky, / OK?

MARK. And now you're here 'cause you had nowhere else to go.

DALE. I'm here 'cause I wanted to see you.

MARK. And 'cause you had no money and nowhere to go –

DALE. I had places to go –

MARK. I'm your last resort.

DALE. No, you're a place I *want* to be. This is where I want to be –

MARK. 'Cause you had nowhere else to go!

DALE. *Damn* right.

You're damn right I had nowhere else to go, I'm on the *street* without you, I had no *house* without you. I'm dead. You *saved* me, OK?

You saved me.

> *(beat)*

MARK. I gotta go to class…

> *(He starts to leave.)*

DALE. Dinner.

Tonight, I'm gonna buy you dinner.

Please.

MARK. I'm back around 7.

Maybe we can go around the corner.

DALE. Great.

That's amazing.

> *(**MARK** turns to leave –)*

Hey, wait a sec.

> *(**DALE** goes to his chest of drawers.)*
>
> *(He pulls out a pair of khakis.)*
>
> *(He holds them out for **MARK**.)*

Check it out.
Dockers.

(They share a look, and **MARK** *leaves.)*

(A long moment.)

*(***DALE*** *goes to the box of stuff.)*

(He sorts through it, piece by piece.)

*(***ECKLAND*** *emerges. He's been in the kitchen the whole time. He and* **DALE** *share a look of understanding.)*

(Lights.)

Scene 15

(Two months later.)

*(**DALE** and **KALINA** stand at the lip of the stage.)*

*(**DALE** wears a suit, nurses a cup of bodega coffee.)*

*(**KALINA** is dressed beautifully, in the orange outfit she'd talked about on the phone.)*

(She holds a scrapbook and looks authentically unlike herself.)

(Like the person she's created.)

(They prepare for a meeting.)

(She speaks in her accent.)

KALINA. September 9th.

DALE. September 9th, yeah.

KALINA. We started talking about the subway lines. Why they are so –

DALE. Why they make no fuckin' sense.

KALINA. Right, yes.

DALE. And you asked me if I was a Republican.

KALINA. Yes, and then you called me a terrorist.

DALE. That was a hypothetical.

KALINA. I suppose.

DALE. Do you still want to do all the stuff about meeting your family? 'Cause I just gotta try to remember all the names.

KALINA. I think that stuff is good.

DALE. I feel a little strange about it, just 'cause –

KALINA. Why do you feel strange?

DALE. I just gotta, um…

Say your mom's name again…?

KALINA. Lamya.

DALE. Lam-ya. Lamya.

KALINA. Will you remember it?

DALE. I'm gonna try.

Maybe they'll laugh if I mess it up.

KALINA. Maybe.

DALE. That seems like a very American thing to do, anyway.

To screw up a Syrian woman's name.

(**KALINA** *smiles.*)

(*beat*)

OK.

Dream vacation: Thailand.

Favorite movie is…what was it. Oh, *Mrs. Doubtfire* / or something?

KALINA. *Mrs. Doubtfire.*

DALE. You want to retire somewhere with seasons.

You usually don't like cooking, but you like making big breakfasts.

You have one tattoo, but your parents don't know.

KALINA. They're not going to ask that.

DALE. I know, I just liked that detail.

KALINA. You could eat a steak any time, for any meal.

Your father worked construction, your mother was a housewife.

You meet up with your best friend from high school every year at a Denny's.

You…once met Johnny Cash. Backstage at a festival. And you didn't know what to say, so you just brought him a drink and you said…

(*She can't remember the words.*)

DALE. 'Thank you.'

KALINA. Thank you. Yes –

DALE. I said thank you and walked away.

Then later that night he walks into our tent. This tiny thing, only like ten of us in there, and we're all playing Stones songs on guitar, The Byrds and shit, tipsy and playing the wrong chords. And he just sits down…

Drinks a beer in the corner.

KALINA. And it's the coolest thing you've ever seen.

> (**DALE** *smiles.*)

DALE. The coolest thing I've ever seen.

KALINA. I feel like I know all these things now...
I feel lucky.
Like now I get the whole *package*. Of you.

DALE. Nah, these are just...plot details.
We don't ever get the whole package.

> (*They look out.*)

KALINA. What do I say about your job if they ask?

DALE. You say I'm a piano teacher.

KALINA. OK.

DALE. That I'm teaching Eckland keyboard. And a couple
classes at this music shop downtown.

KALINA. That's fun.

DALE. Yeah, you know.
It's something.

> (*beat*)

KALINA. You're saving me.
And I'm very grateful to you.

DALE. I'm glad I can help.

KALINA. You're a good person.

DALE. Not really.
No.
...
But it's nice that you think so.

> (*They stand and face out.*)

> (*blackout*)

End of Play